KT-458-197

Enid Blyton

THE SECRET SEVEN

THE HUMBUG ADVENTURE

Illustrated by Tony Ross

Hodder
Children's
Books

THE SECRET SEVEN

PETER   JANET   JACK   COLIN

GEORGE   PAM   BARBARA

Have you read them all?

ADVENTURE ON THE WAY HOME

THE HUMBUG ADVENTURE

AN AFTERNOON WITH THE SECRET SEVEN

WHERE ARE THE SECRET SEVEN?

HURRY, SECRET SEVEN, HURRY!

THE SECRET OF OLD MILL

... now try the full-length **SECRET SEVEN** mysteries:

THE SECRET SEVEN

SECRET SEVEN ADVENTURE

WELL DONE, SECRET SEVEN

SECRET SEVEN ON THE TRAIL

GO AHEAD, SECRET SEVEN

GOOD WORK, SECRET SEVEN

SECRET SEVEN WIN THROUGH

THREE CHEERS, SECRET SEVEN

SECRET SEVEN MYSTERY

PUZZLE FOR THE SECRET SEVEN

SECRET SEVEN FIREWORKS

GOOD OLD SECRET SEVEN

SHOCK FOR THE SECRET SEVEN

LOOK OUT, SECRET SEVEN

FUN FOR THE SECRET SEVEN

SCAMPER

HODDER CHILDREN'S BOOKS

Text first published in Great Britain in 1954 in *Enid Blyton's Magazine Annual 1*
This edition first published in 2016 by Hodder & Stoughton

3 5 7 9 10 8 6 4

The Secret Seven®, Enid Blyton® and Enid Blyton's signature are
Registered Trademarks of Hodder & Stoughton Limited
Text © Hodder & Stoughton Limited
Illustrations © Hodder & Stoughton Limited
No trademark or copyrighted material may be reproduced without the express written
permission of the trademark and copyright owner

All of the moral rights of Enid Blyton and Tony Ross are hereby asserted.

All characters and events in this publication, other than those clearly
in the public domain, are fictitious and any resemblance to
real persons, living or dead, is purely coincidental.

All rights reserved.
No part of this publication may be reproduced, stored in
a retrieval system, or transmitted, in any form or by any means, without
the prior permission in writing of the publisher, nor be otherwise circulated
in any form of binding or cover other than that in which it is published
and without a similar condition including this condition being
imposed on the subsequent purchaser.

A CIP catalogue record for this book is available from the British Library.

ISBN 978 1 444 92766 5

Printed and bound in China

The paper and board used in this book are made from wood from responsible sources.

Hodder Children's Books
An imprint of
Hachette Children's Group
Part of Hodder and Stoughton
Carmelite House
50 Victoria Embankment
London EC4Y 0DZ

An Hachette UK Company
www.hachette.co.uk
www.hachettechildrens.co.uk

CHAPTER ONE

The Secret Seven met one day after morning school. 'What about this invitation from old Professor Wills to go and look at the planet Jupiter tonight

through his telescope?' said
Peter. 'I don't know why he's
picked on us to ask!'

'I've already seen it on
television,' said Colin. 'There
wasn't much to see!'

'It'll be awfully boring,'
said Jack. 'He's not a bit
interesting. He just drones on
and on. Let's not go.'

'Well – wouldn't it be
rude if we all left messages to

say we weren't coming?' asked Janet. 'After all – he means it kindly. And he has got a jolly big telescope!'

'It's going to rain,' said Pam, looking up at the sky. 'I bet it is. So we shan't see a thing if we do go!'

'If it rains, we won't go,' said Peter. 'So we'll just hope that it pours and pours!'

CHAPTER TWO

It didn't. The sky was certainly cloudy, but no rain came at all. The Seven sighed as they ate their tea in their different homes. They would have to go after all!

So they went, waiting for each other outside Professor Wills's house, which was called 'Night Skies'. That made them laugh. At last each member was there, and in they went.

The maid showed them into a study, and then went to fetch the old professor. She came back looking sorry.

'It's such a cloudy night

that the professor didn't expect you,' she said. 'So he's gone out. But his wife says that if you are very, very careful, she will show you how to work the telescope and you can see if you can spy Jupiter for yourselves. Ah – here she comes.'

Mrs Wills was very nice. To begin with she produced a tin of most enormous humbugs to suck. Then she showed

Peter and the others how to train the big telescope on to different points of the sky.

'I know just about where the planet Jupiter is,' she said, 'and if you like, I'll leave the telescope pointed at the place it should be, behind the clouds. Then, when the clouds move on, you may catch a glimpse of it now and then.'

CHAPTER THREE

None of the Secret Seven
could speak a word because
of the big humbugs they were
sucking. Peter made some
polite noises, and hoped that

Mrs Wills understood. When she had gone out of the room, the Seven looked at each other in relief.

'**Ooogle, elescopy-oogle, urble, oopiter**,' said Peter. Nobody understood. He put his eye to the end of the great tube and looked up.

'**Uthing ooing**,' he said, which the others correctly understood as 'Nothing doing.'

Jack worked his humbug round to the other side of his mouth.

'**Urgle, onky, ooky ky**,' he said, meaning, 'Let's not look at the sky,' but nobody understood a word! So he took his humbug out of his mouth and explained:

'Let's not bother about looking at the cloudy sky,' he said clearly. 'Let's bend the telescope down a bit and look at the village and the hills beyond and the farm – things like that. It would be fun to stand here, far away from them, and see them almost as if we could touch them!'

'Yes, let's,' said Peter. 'We know how to move the telescope. But for goodness' sake be careful, it's jolly valuable.'

CHAPTER FOUR

The telescope had a curious
window of its own to look
through – a great window that
reached from ceiling almost
to ground, and had no glass

in at all. It could be swung to almost any angle at a touch of the finger once a screw had been loosened.

'Let's look at the Village Hall,' said Janet. 'There's a dance on and it's all lit up.' She had taken her humbug out of her mouth to speak, and put it back again when she had finished. Peter was afraid of sticky finger marks on

the telescope, and he handed Colin a clean hanky to wipe where anyone touched.

The Village Hall looked so near that it might have been in the garden. Barbara took her sweet out of her mouth and giggled. 'There's Mrs Dickson, look, standing at the door. And do look, there's that silly boy Harry selling programmes or something.'

This was a marvellous game! They moved the telescope into another direction, and saw where a fair was, in the farmer's field about a quarter of a mile away.

'Goodness – it looks so near that I'm sure I heard that roundabout man **sneeze**!' said Janet. 'And I can even see Dickie and

Danny, the twins, paying their pennies to go on together!'

They spent a long time looking at the fair, and began to wish they were there.

CHAPTER FIVE

'**Urgle, ooble, oo**,' said Peter, forgetting to take out his humbug, but the others knew what he meant, because he was swinging the telescope slowly to a different direction. It was now pointing towards the dark farm. One window was brilliantly lit and no curtains were drawn.

'There's nice Mrs Wingfield knitting in her chair,' said Barbara, taking her turn.

'And old Mr Wingfield filling his pipe,' said Colin. 'I can even see what tobacco he's using!'

'You *can't*,' said everyone, mumbling.

Then it was Jack's turn. He bent and looked through the great tube, seeing the farm itself and the barn nearby and a haystack. He suddenly gave a loud exclamation, and most unexpectedly swallowed his humbug. He gasped and choked, tried to call out something and pointed to the telescope.

In astonishment, Peter looked through it. What was Jack fussing about?

He soon saw! Someone was moving near the haystack. Someone was striking matches! Little flames sprang up in the dry stack, and soon there were many more. Peter **gasped**, not taking any notice of poor, choking Jack. His eye was glued to the big telescope.

He squashed his humbug into his cheek in order to speak clearly. '**Fire**! There's a tramp setting fire to Farmer Wingfield's stack – and it's jolly near the old barn. Gosh, that's a big flame! Colin, go and ring up the farmer – at once! And, after that, the police. The stack will soon be burnt down, then the barn will catch fire!'

CHAPTER SIX

Colin ran to find the
telephone in the hall.
Peter had his eye glued to
the telescope, watching
everything. There was the man

again, coming from behind the stack. He had probably set fire to the other side too! Peter could see him clearly – a small man, with a limp and a beard that showed up well when he turned sideways to the flames. Janet tried to pull her brother away so that she could have a turn herself, but he wouldn't budge.

Colin telephoned the

farm and gave them a warning. Then he got on to the police. He ran back into the telescope room. 'Peter, I've phoned! What's happening now?'

Peter was having a most wonderful view of all the sudden excitement at the farm. The farm door was flung open, and out ran the farmer and his son. His wife followed with buckets.

A minute later the police came up in a car. Then firemen, called by the police, arrived too. What a to-do! Peter gasped and exclaimed, and the others could hardly contain themselves!

'Let's have a look, Peter! Peter, you selfish thing, let *us* have a turn. **What's happening**?'

Peter told them.

'Everyone's arrived – the stack's blazing, but the barn is safe. The firemen are drenching the stack now – and goodness, they've caught the man. **No – it's not him**. The man who set fire to the stack was small and had a beard and a limp. They've got the wrong man – no wonder he's struggling!'

CHAPTER SEVEN

This was too much for the others. They raced out of the room together. 'We're going to the farm! It's too thrilling for words!'

So down to the farm they went, and managed to see the end of the excitement. Half the stack was saved – the barn was not touched – and a man was trying to get away from two stout policemen.

'I didn't set fire to it, I tell you!' he was shouting.

Jack went up to the sergeant, who was standing

nearby. 'Sir – I don't think that man did do it,' he said. 'The man you want has a limp – he's small – and has a beard.'

'Why – that would be Jamey!' cried the farmer's wife. 'We sent him off last week for stealing.'

The police let the other man go. The sergeant ordered them to go to

Jamey's cottage, not far off. Then he turned to Jack. 'Now perhaps you'll tell us how you know all this, you kids?' he said with his large smile. 'Warned the farmer – called the police – and even know who the man is who set fire to the stack! You're the Secret Seven, aren't you? Always into something, I know!'

'We saw it all through

Professor Wills's telescope,'
said Jack. 'Peter's still back
there, watching.'

But he wasn't.

CHAPTER EIGHT

As soon as Peter saw the
others through the telescope,
appearing in the midst of the
excitement, he wanted to be
with them – and he ran at top

speed, sucking the very last of his humbug!

'Good work,' said the sergeant, when Peter told the whole of the story. 'You saw something more exciting than the planet Jupiter, didn't you? Ah – you never know what you're going to see through telescopes.'

'It was a jolly good adventure, but a very sudden

and short one,' said Colin.

'Yes,' said Peter. 'It only lasted as long as my humbug. An adventure *couldn't* very well be shorter than that!'

'Short and sweet – like the humbug,' said Janet with a giggle. 'Let's call it the Humbug Adventure – it's a jolly good name for it!'

So it is – don't you agree?

LOOK OUT FOR ANOTHER
SECRET SEVEN
COLOUR SHORT STORY ...

ADVENTURE ON THE WAY HOME

A big fight has broken out, and the Seven make it their mission to put a stop to it before someone gets hurt. But what's really going on between the angry people?

LOOK OUT FOR ANOTHER
SECRET SEVEN
COLOUR SHORT STORY ...

AN AFTERNOON WITH THE SECRET SEVEN

Peter is manning the hoopla stall at the fair, but when Fred offers him a pony ride, he can't resist. Scamper is left in charge. But when Peter returns, Scamper and the money are missing! What's been going on?

LOOK OUT FOR A FULL-LENGTH

SECRET SEVEN

MYSTERY ...

Well Done, Secret Seven

The Secret Seven have a new meeting place - a tree-house! But someone else is using it too. The gang are furious, but then they learn the intruder is in big trouble, and needs their help. Can the Seven come to the rescue?

THE SECRET SEVEN
COLOUR SHORT STORIES

enidblyton.co.uk